IN HONOR OF

Pat Foster

For Rubin and Mara, with love. —P. M.

To all the children fighting and caring
for our friend Earth. —F. S.

My Friend Earth

written by Patricia MacLachlan

illustrated by Francesca Sanna

chronicle books · san francisco

My friend Earth wakes
from a winter nap.

She hears the busy spring sounds—
the farmer's hoe tap-tapping in the garden,

the caws of crows.

She sees the little—

the silent seed,
the spider spinning silver,
the robin and the wrens.

And the large—

the long-winged albatross   crossing the sea,

the mole tunneling in the underdark.

She guides the chimpanzee
to her night nest—

and the zebra baby to find his mother

in the hundreds
of black-and-white striped mothers.

She tends the prairie where sun-dappled wild horses run

through grasses that swish against their legs—

the tundra
where the reindeer
graze for moss,

and the glistening ice
where the young polar bear
pads on mittened feet.

She guards all the creatures in all the oceans—
the black manta rays sleek like shadows,

the shining parrot fish,
the tiny krill who swim with millions of other krill to look big.

And the whales
who **are** big.

My friend Earth
pours the summer rain
to fill streams

flowing down mountains

through the fields

to the rivers

to the sea.

Sometimes she pours too much rain,

flooding towns
and meadows

and roads.

Until she dries the land.

Sometimes she blows fierce autumn winds,
sweeping the limbs of trees
and shingles from the roofs of barns.

Until she stills the wind,

so red and orange and yellow leaves
float to the ground.

When cold comes again,
my friend Earth sprinkles the snow—
whisper silent—

covering the dens where
the baby black bears are born
in soft darkness,

pond where the turtle sleeps in mud,
to the empty nests of birds.

Under the

the silent see

is cradled in the d

Watching.

Waiting.

To fly up again in the warm bright sun of spring!

PATRICIA MacLACHLAN is an acclaimed author who has written dozens of books—including the Newbery Medal–winner *Sarah, Plain and Tall* and the Barkus series, also published by Chronicle Books. She lives in Massachusetts.

FRANCESCA SANNA grew up on the Italian island of Sardinia. She studied illustration at the School of Visual Arts in New York and the Academy of Art and Design in Lucerne. Francesca currently lives in Zurich, but you can visit her at Francescasanna.com.

ALSO BY PATRICIA MacLACHLAN

BARKUS
★ "A top pick."—*School Library Journal*, starred review

THE IRIDESCENCE OF BIRDS: A BOOK ABOUT HENRI MATISSE
★ "Glorious."—*Kirkus Reviews*, starred review

SNOWFLAKES FALL
★ "[A] hopeful, uplifting book."—*Booklist*, starred review

THE MOON'S ALMOST HERE
★ "Lullaby-like verse."—*Publishers Weekly*, starred review

ALSO BY FRANCESCA SANNA

THE JOURNEY
A New York Times Notable Children's Book
A Wall Street Journal Best Children's Book
A Publishers Weekly Best Book
A Kirkus Reviews Best Children's Book
A School Library Journal Best Children's Book
A Guardian Best Children's Book

Text copyright © 2020 by Patricia MacLachlan.

Illustrations copyright © 2020 by Francesca Sanna.

Library of Congress Cataloging-in-Publication Data available.

ISBN 978-0-8118-7910-1

Manufactured in China.

MIX
Paper from
responsible sources
FSC™ C008047

Design by Sara Gillingham Studio.

Typeset in Sonopa.

The illustrations in this book were rendered in pencil, ink, and digital painting.

10 9 8 7 6

Chronicle Books LLC

680 Second Street, San Francisco, California 94107

Chronicle Books—we see things differently. Become part of our community at www.chroniclekids.com.